Prison Satellite

Leo P. Kelley

A SPACE POLICE BOOK

HUTCHINSON

London Melbourne Sydney Auckland Johannesburg

The SPACE POLICE™ Series

Prison Satellite
Worlds Apart
Earth Two

Backward in Time
Sunworld
Death Sentence

Editorial Director: Robert G. Bander
Managing Designer: Kauthar Hawkins
Cover illustrator: Steven Hofheimer

Hutchinson and Co. (Publishers) Ltd
An imprint of the Hutchinson Publishing Group
24 Highbury Crescent, London N5 1RX

Hutchinson Group (Australia) Pty Ltd
30-32 Cremorne Street, Richmond South, Victoria 3121
PO Box 151, Broadway, New South Wales 2007

Hutchinson Group (NZ) Ltd
32-34 View Road, PO Box 40-086, Glenfield, Auckland 10

Hutchinson Group (SA) (Pty) Ltd
PO Box 337, Bergvlei 2012, South Africa

First published in Great Britain 1980
Hutchinson and Co. (Publishers) Ltd

Printed in the United States of America

ISBN-0-09-142131-4

CONTENTS

A NEW JOB FOR BARRY

His name was Barry Marks. He had been Officer Barry Marks of the Space Police for a year. He had a square face, blue eyes, and dark hair that was almost black. When he smiled, which was often, he looked more like a boy than a man.

After finishing his police training, Barry had worked on Earth. But now he worked on the planet Delta, which was far away from Earth.

Barry was in the police station on Delta, sitting at a table across from his partner,

Dennis Vilma. He looked down at the cards he held in his hand.

Some were square and some were round. All but one were blue. That one was red. On the faces of the cards were pictures—pictures of laser guns, spaceships, people, stars, planets, and computers.

Barry played two of his cards. One was blue and had a picture of a spaceship on it. The other was the red one with a picture of a star on it. Barry looked up at Dennis.

But Dennis didn't look at him. He kept his eyes on the cards he held in his hand. He ran his hand through his hair and then picked out one of his cards. It was a square blue one, with a picture of a man on it. He put it on the table next to Barry's two cards. Then he took a round red card from his hand. The card had a picture of a computer on it. He placed this card on the table, too.

"Got you that time," Dennis said. "The man uses the computer to stop your spaceship from reaching your star. He puts your ship out of order with the help of the computer. That move gives me the game."

Barry threw down the rest of his cards and sat back in his chair. He shook his head. "How do you do it, Dennis? You win every time. What do you do—cheat?"

Dennis burst out laughing. "Who, me? Are you kidding? I don't have to cheat. I'm a good card player, that's all. And if I did cheat, do you think I'd tell you?"

Dennis began to pick up the cards. He asked Barry, "Want to try again? Do you still think you can beat me?"

Before Barry could answer him, the voice of the computer that stood next to the wall spoke out.

"Officers Marks and Vilma," said the computer. "You are to go to City Factory. A fight is taking place there. You are to break it up."

Barry was on his feet at once and headed for the door. Dennis was right behind him. The two officers jumped into their Air Car and flew to City Factory.

When they reached the big building that was City Factory, they went inside. Loud noise met their ears. A fight was taking place, just as the police computer had said. Metal machines of all kinds were fighting each other.

A small square machine ran about on its one wheel, banging into other machines. After it hit another machine, it rolled away as fast as it could. In a corner of the room, two big machines with long metal arms were hitting each other. Across the room a three-sided machine with clocks on each of its sides ran along its metal track. Little yellow lights flashed on it as it knocked other machines out of its way. Then it turned and went back the way it had come.

"Police officers!" Barry shouted at the top of his voice. *"Stop your fighting!"* But his words were lost in the loud noise the machines were making.

He shouted a second time. Still the fighting didn't stop. None of the machines seemed to have heard him. Even if they had heard him, they kept on fighting with each other.

Barry fired his laser gun into the air.

All the machines stopped moving.

Barry, with Dennis at his side, moved in among them.

He asked, "Now just what's this all about? Who started this fight? And why?"

The three-sided clock-faced machine rolled forward on its track. When it reached Barry, it spoke. Its voice sounded like glass breaking. "I have a Class Six brain. I'm in control of this factory. Just now some of these other machines tried to take over the factory. But not one of them has more than a Class Four brain!"

Barry asked, "So you tried to stop them, is that it?"

"Of course I did," said the machine. "Me and the machines that are on my side."

Barry asked another question. "Why did the other machines try to take over the factory?"

A machine with six metal legs moved forward and shouted, "I'm a Class Three brain. But that Class Six there won't let me or any of the other Threes do any interesting work. I can, you know. My Class Three brain is good enough for lots of different jobs."

With that, the machines began to fight again.

Barry grabbed the machine nearest to him. He pressed the Off button on the side of the machine. It stopped fighting. It didn't move. It couldn't. Then, together, Barry and Dennis went after the other machines. One by one they turned them all off. When all was quiet, Barry turned the three-sided clock-faced machine back on.

The machine looked around and said, "What happened? Am I out of order?"

"I'll say you're out of order," said Dennis. "But not the way you mean."

Then Barry spoke to the machine. "Now you listen to me for a minute. I want you to let these other machines work on things their brains are right for. If you don't I'll arrest you for fighting. And you know what that will mean."

The machine backed away from Barry. "Don't arrest me. Please don't. If I'm arrested, I'll be turned off for good!"

"That's right," said Dennis.

"You got it," said Barry.

"But I'm a Class Six brain!" said the machine. "These other machines aren't nearly as clever as I am."

"It's up to you," said Barry. "What's it going to be?"

The machine turned this way and that. Its little yellow lights flashed on and off. Then it said, "You win. I'll let the other machines work on interesting things, too. But I have to say that it's a sad day when a Class Six brain can't run things its own way."

A few minutes later, all the machines were back at work. When peace had returned to the factory, Barry and Dennis started back to the station in their Air Car. But before they got there, the voice of the police computer came through their radio.

"Officers Marks and Vilma. A child is missing. Please look into the matter at once."

Since the computer stored the names and addresses of all the people living on Delta, it was able to give Barry and Dennis the information they needed. It gave them the child's name and the address of her home. It also flashed a picture of the missing child on the Air Car's TV set. When all the necessary information was given, Barry turned the Air Car around and headed at top speed for the house.

The child's mother was waiting for the officers when they got there. Barry could see that the woman had been crying. He asked her some questions. She told him that she was sure her little girl had run away.

Barry asked, "Why would she do that?"

"Because she wanted a Jet-Pack so she could fly around in the park down the road," the mother answered. "I told her she couldn't have one. I was afraid she might hurt herself. She got very cross at me. And now she hasn't come home from school and I can't find her!"

"She might be somewhere in your house," Dennis said. "She might be hiding from you."

"Let's go in and look around," Barry said.

He and Dennis went into the house. They looked everywhere but they didn't find the girl. They did find a toy bank in the girl's room. It was broken and empty.

Outside again, Barry told Dennis and the girl's mother that he'd be back soon. Then he asked Dennis to take a quick look around the streets.

As Barry got into their Air Car, Dennis asked, "Where are you going?"

"I've got an idea," Barry said. Then he flew away.

Soon he was back. The little girl was with him.

When the mother saw her daughter, she said, "Oh, where have you been?" She threw her arms around the girl.

The girl said, "After school I went to the Jet-Pack shop. I broke into my toy bank this morning so I could buy myself a Jet-Pack."

Just then Dennis returned. He saw the girl with Barry. He asked, "Where did you find her?"

"At the Jet-Pack shop, just where I thought she'd be," he answered.

"You're too young to fly," the mother told her daughter.

"Jet-Packs are safe," Barry said. "And your daughter looks old enough to fly. I'd say that she's about 12 years old."

"I'll soon be 13," said the girl. She smiled up at Barry.

"Well, promise me that you'll be very careful," said the mother.

The girl promised. Then Barry helped her put on the Jet-Pack. The girl flew up into the air and around in a circle. She laughed and waved to the three people watching her. Everyone waved back. Then Barry and Dennis got back into their Air Car.

As soon as they got to the station, the computer spoke Barry's name.

Barry thought to himself, what now?

The computer said, "Officer Barry Marks is to begin a new job tomorrow. Officer Marks will go to work on the prison satellite."

"Oh, no!" Barry said. "That's the last job in the galaxy I ever want."

Dennis asked, "What's wrong with working on the prison satellite? I hear it's a pretty soft job."

"That's the trouble," Barry said. "Nothing ever happens there."

But he was wrong. And he'd soon find out how wrong.

PRISONERS IN SPACE

When he woke up the next day, the first thing Barry thought of was to ask for his old job back. He really didn't want to work on the prison satellite. He wanted an interesting job—one that kept him out on the streets where things were always going on. A job that he could enjoy because there was something new and different every day.

But he knew that he should take the new job he had been given. Not just because he had been ordered to take it, but also because he wanted to learn about all kinds of police work.

The more he knew, the better his chances were for making his dream come true. That dream was to become a commander in the Space Police force one day.

So Barry got up and dressed and went to the police ship that was to take him to the prison satellite. After an hour of flying through deep space, the ship reached the satellite. Barry looked at it through the ship's windows.

It was by far the biggest satellite of its kind that he had ever seen. It was shaped like three balls set on top of each other. The biggest ball was at the bottom. The smallest was on top. To fly, the satellite used power it took from a sun. There were three big letters on the side of the bottom circle: *SPF.* Everyone in space knew that those letters stood for Space Police Force.

The police ship docked with the satellite and Barry went on board. He went at once to the satellite's commander's officer. He knocked on the door. A voice behind the door told him to come in.

Commander Ruth Olinda was looking through some papers on her desk as Barry

walked in. She looked up at Barry and returned his salute. Then she told him to sit
down.

"You have a fine record, Officer Marks," she
said. "That's good. In fact that's why I asked to
have you sent here. I want only the best police
officers in my command."

"Thank you," Barry said. He watched her as
she spoke. She had clear brown eyes and short
brown hair. She seemed very sure of herself
but she looked young to be the commander of a
prison satellite. Barry knew, though, that age
wasn't the important thing in getting to be a
commander. Working hard and doing your job
well were all that mattered.

"That's about all I have to say for now,"
Commander Olinda said a few minutes later.
"I'm glad to have you in my command, Officer
Marks."

Barry stood up. Then Commander Olinda
pressed a button on her desk. "I'll get Officer
Tarkoff to show you round the prison. She'll
answer any questions you may have. Take
today off. Look around. Get to know the place.
You'll begin work tomorrow."

The office door opened and a woman came in.

"This is Officer Joan Tarkoff," Commander Olinda said. Barry said good-bye to the Commander and left the office with Joan Tarkoff.

"I hope you'll like it here," Joan said as she led the way down a long hall. "Commander Olinda is hard on people. But she's fair."

"I have the feeling she asks a lot of everyone who works for her," Barry told her.

"She only asks us to follow the rules and do our jobs the way they're supposed to be done. So don't worry. I'm sure you'll have no trouble," Joan answered.

"I hope I don't," Barry said. He looked at Joan Tarkoff as they walked along. She moved fast and yet she didn't seem to rush. Her hair was black, and her eyes were dark brown. She looked you in the eye when she talked.

Joan took Barry to the top part of the prison first. She showed him where the officers lived. Each officer had a small but nice room. Then she led Barry down some stairs and into a large room. There was the biggest computer he had ever seen in his life. It almost filled the room.

"Meet the Judge," Joan said. She pointed to the computer.

Barry had heard about the computer that judged all criminal cases. But he had never seen it before. He knew that the lawyers put into the computer all the facts for and against a person held for a crime. So did all the witnesses in the case. So did the police who had made the arrest. Then the computer checked all the facts against the laws it knew. And then it decided if the person accused of the crime was guilty or innocent.

Barry looked at the machine. "I made a few arrests in my time which that computer threw out. The criminals went free."

"It happens," Joan said. "But the computer knows everything about all the laws there are. You and I don't. Oh, we know a lot, of course. But the computer knows more than we do. So some of our arrests won't turn out the way we think they will."

Joan led the way out of the room and down to the bottom of the satellite. "This is where the prisoners live," she said. "Some of them are waiting for the computer to decide if they are guilty or innocent. Others are here to do their time."

Joan led Barry past many cells where prisoners were being held. The cells were made of glass that couldn't be broken. Some of the cells were filled with a strange kind of gas because there were aliens in those cells who couldn't breathe air. Other glass-walled cells were filled with red water. There were aliens in those cells who could live only in the strange red water of their home worlds.

Suddenly a green light began to flash.

"That means the computer has just decided a case," Joan told Barry.

The voice of the computer came through the speakers on the walls. "I have found prisoner 59013AA guilty of murder. Prisoner 59013AA will be executed for his crime."

Far down the row of cells, a man began to sing at the top of his voice.

"That's prisoner 59013AA," Joan told Barry.

"Why is he singing? If he's going to be executed, I'd say he's got nothing to sing about."

"He's probably trying to act as if he doesn't care," Joan said. Then she added, "He was arrested for murder . . . on the planet Delta."

"Delta? That's where I come from." Barry walked down to the cell where the singing was coming from. He stopped and looked inside.

The prisoner stopped singing. He looked out at Barry. Then he said, "Well, look who's here. If it isn't my old friend from the wrong side of the law. How are you, cop?"

"I'm OK, Kirkland."

"Aren't you going to ask me how I am?"

Barry said nothing.

"I'm not so good," Kirkland said. "You can't feel too good when you know you're going to go sailing out into space. And, what's more, without a spacesuit to keep out the cold and give you a little air to breathe. No, cop, I'm not so good at all."

Barry asked, "Who did you kill, Kirkland?"

"Go away, cop. I don't want to talk to you. Get out."

Barry turned away from the cell and went back to where Joan was waiting for him. "I know him," he told her. "I arrested Kirkland twice on Delta. But that was for little crimes. I never thought that he would kill anyone."

"Well, he did, and the computer says he must die for his crime."

"When?"

"In three days," Joan said. "Every execution takes place three days after the computer decides the case."

Barry said, "Who executes the prisoner?"

"One of us," Joan said. "We take it in turn."

Barry looked toward Kirkland's cell and then back at Joan. "Who's going to execute Kirkland?"

"We can find out," Joan said. She took Barry to a room at one end of the cellblock. On a wall was a long list. "The name of the executing officer will be on this list."

Barry took the list from her. On it were the names of all the officers in the prison. It showed what each officer's job was for each day.

Barry looked through the list for the day of Kirkland's execution. Then he saw his name. He was the one who was to execute Kirkland.

KIRKLAND'S ATOMIC MACHINE

The next day—his first on the job—Barry was put in control of the cellblock. He saw to it that the prisoners were given their food on time. He let the human prisoners out of their cells so they could move around a little. He saw to it that the gas and the red water in the aliens' cells were changed.

One thing he did not do. He did not go near Kirkland's cell. He didn't want to see the man—he didn't even want to think about him. He also didn't want to think about what he would have to do to Kirkland in two more days.

But that thought wouldn't go away. It kept coming back. In two more days Barry would press a button outside Kirkland's cell. A wall would come down behind the bars. Kirkland's cell would be shut off completely from the rest of the prison. Then Barry would press a second button. The wall at the far end of Kirkland's cell would open. Kirkland would float out into space where there was no air to breathe. In minutes he would be dead. His body would float among the stars. But his eyes would never see them again.

The day passed. The next day came.

Barry couldn't stop thinking about Kirkland. In the end, he went to the man's cell. When he got there he said, "OK, Kirkland. What happened? Who did you kill?"

Barry thought Kirkland would tell him to go away. But he didn't. Instead he came to the bars of his cell and looked out at Barry. Then he said, "These last few days I've been doing a lot of hard thinking, cop."

"I know." Barry asked his questions a second time.

Suddenly Kirkland started talking. He seemed to be trying to tell Barry the story of his life as fast as he could. So Barry listened.

"At first it was just like a game," Kirkland said. "I stole and I got away with it. Then I tried for something bigger. I got it too. It was fun. It made me feel I was a very big man. Other people worked at their jobs. Then they went home. Their life was nothing to them, you know? But me, I lived very high. Nothing could touch me. Not the people all around me and not the law either."

"I got you twice, Kirkland," Barry said. "Once for stealing clothes and once for trying to rob a bank."

Kirkland laughed. "So what happened, cop? You remember what happened, don't you?"

"The computer set you free. You had a good lawyer."

Kirkland grabbed the bars of his cell. "You want to know something mad?" He didn't wait for Barry to answer him. "I'm glad it's finally over. I really am. Funny, isn't it? I'm sure you never thought you'd hear me say that. Well, it's true. After I killed that woman, it was all over for me. I didn't mean to kill her. But she jumped up and started screaming. I lost my head. I fired. And she was dead—just like that.

I couldn't believe it. I went to pieces. That killing also killed something in me. I wanted to die after that."

Barry asked, "How did it happen?"

"I was on the run from the cops. I hijacked a ship that was about to make the trip from Delta to Earth. A woman on the ship got scared. She started screaming and running at me. After I shot her I froze. Somebody grabbed my gun and it was all over."

Kirkland looked down at the floor and then up at Barry. "I've got a younger brother named Morgan. That kid thinks I'm the greatest. He always has. I tell him he's all wrong. I tell him I'm nothing but a loser. But he never believes me. Cop, I worry about what's going to happen to Morgan when I'm gone."

Barry could think of nothing to say.

"Morgan's clever," Kirkland went on. "He's too clever for his own good sometimes. I really worry about him. I don't care about myself any more. Perhaps I never did when you come down to it. But the kid—Morgan's still in the clear. But I don't think he's going to stay that way. He wants to be like me, he says. I don't want him to be like me. I took my chances and I lost, so I'm going to get what's coming to me. But then my brother won't have anyone left to keep him on the right track. We only have each other."

Barry looked at his watch. "I've got to go now, Kirkland. It's five minutes to lights out. Why don't you try to take it easy?"

"Oh, sure, I'll take it easy. Nice and easy." Kirkland began to laugh as Barry walked away.

That night Barry dreamed that he was all by himself in Kirkland's cell. Kirkland stood outside it. He was laughing. His finger was on the button. He pressed it. Barry asked him not to touch the other button. But then the cell opened to let in the stars. Barry woke up feeling as cold as ice.

That day was visiting day. Ships came, and humans and aliens came into the prison. Before they got to the cellblock, police officers made the visitors walk slowly past a machine that would find any metal they had on them. But none of them had guns. After they were checked the visitors were taken to the cellblock. An officer stood outside each cell, watching the prisoners and the visitors.

Barry's job was to watch Kirkland. Kirkland's younger brother, Morgan, came and Barry let him into Kirkland's cell. He stood outside, watching the two men as he was supposed to do. He couldn't hear what they were saying because they whispered.

After a few minutes Kirkland looked at Barry. He waved a hand. Barry didn't move. Then Kirkland said, "Go away, will you, cop?" He looked sad.

Barry thought for a second, then he walked away from the cell. He knew he wasn't supposed to leave when a visitor was in the cell. But he was sure that Kirkland was about to cry. And he knew that Kirkland wouldn't want Barry to see him cry. He waited for five minutes. Then, just as he was about to go back to the cell, he heard noises coming from it.

He ran up the hall. When he got to the cell, he looked inside. Kirkland was hitting his brother. Barry took out his key, opened the cell door, and ran inside. He pulled Kirkland away from his brother.

"Get out of here," he told Morgan. Morgan left quickly. Then Barry looked hard at Kirkland and asked, "What did you hit him for?"

Kirkland's eyes looked dead. He shook his head slowly from side to side. He said something, but Barry caught only two words—". . . family fight."

Barry left the cell and locked it. He looked at Morgan, who stood outside the cell. "You'd better leave now," he said. Morgan left. An hour later, all the visitors had gone.

Soon, everything was quiet.

Barry walked down the hall, checking each cell. Suddenly, there was a loud noise and a flash of light. Barry stopped in his tracks as the door of Kirkland's cell blew open. Kirkland came out of his cell. He held a small red machine. Barry reached for his laser gun.

"Hold it," Kirkland ordered him. "If you try to use that gun I'll blow the whole place up. Hand it over."

Barry gave Kirkland his gun.

"Now that's better," said Kirkland. "That's fine." In one hand he held Barry's gun. In his other hand he held his red machine.

Kirkland smiled. "I told you my kid brother is smart. He made this machine. He slipped it to me when he was in my cell. I put it under my bed so you wouldn't spot it. That's why I wanted you to go away—so Morgan would hand this over to me."

Barry asked, "That machine—is that what you used on your cell door?"

"Yes. It's like a little atomic bomb—and it's under my control. I used only a small part of its power on the cell door. Now, cop, I want you to do something for me—or else I'll have to use this thing again."

Then Kirkland told Barry what he wanted him to do.

At first, Barry said he wouldn't do it. But then Kirkland pointed out to him that if he didn't, he'd die. So would all the other prisoners and police officers on the satellite.

"You'll die too, Kirkland," Barry said. But as soon as he said the words, he knew he had lost the game.

"I'm going to die tomorrow anyhow, if I don't get out of here," Kirkland said. "So I've got nothing to lose. Now do what I told you."

Barry spoke slowly into one of the speakers on the wall. "This is Officer Marks. We have a problem in the cellblock. An escaped prisoner."

Kirkland screamed at him, "Tell them what I want!"

"Prisoner 59013AA has escaped from his cell. He has an atomic machine that can blow up the prison and everyone in it."

"The ship!" Kirkland shouted.

"The prisoner wants a police ship to fly him out of here."

For several seconds there was no sound in the cellblock. The other prisoners watched Barry and Kirkland. Finally Commander Olinda's voice came over the wall speakers.

"Marks, how did the prisoner get the atomic machine?"

"It's not made of metal," Barry answered. "The prisoner's brother just visited him and gave him the machine. It would not have shown up when the prisoner's brother went through the metal check."

"That is not what I wanted to know," said Commander Olinda. "You were watching the prisoner and his visitor. How could the visitor have given the prisoner the machine without you seeing it?"

Barry looked at Kirkland. Kirkland smiled.

Barry said, "I was away from the cell for five minutes, Commander."

"Say that again, Marks." Commander Olinda's voice was cold.

Barry told her that he had left the prisoner's cell for five minutes during the visit.

"Listen to me!" Kirkland shouted then. "Forget Marks. I want that police ship and I want it now! Do you hear me?"

"Yes. I'll get back to you in a little while," Commander Olinda said.

"It better be a *very* little while!" Kirkland called out. "If you don't get me that ship, you'll be burnt up with everyone else in this zoo!"

THE FIRST ESCAPE

Barry asked Kirkland, "What do you want a police ship for? Why not take a one-man ship that *you* can fly?"

"And have all the police ships in this part of space come after me? Use your head, cop. If I leave in a police ship, with a police officer at the controls, I'm safe. I've got my machine. I could blow up the ship. And the cop flying it. So the other ships will stay far away from me."

Barry said, "You've thought it all out, haven't you?" He was watching Kirkland and waiting for the man to make a wrong move. If

Kirkland did, Barry would be able to get him.

"That's right, cop. I've thought the whole thing out."

"What about Morgan, Kirkland? You know we'll get him for helping you to escape. I thought you wanted the kid to stay clean."

Kirkland's face grew dark. He looked away from Barry. Barry took a quick step toward him. But Kirkland turned back fast.

"Don't move another step," he told Barry.

Barry didn't move. He said, "You'll never get away from here, Kirkland. And what's more, you'll soon have company. Once we take care of you, we'll go after Morgan and bring him here, too. That should make you very happy."

"Shut up!" Kirkland shouted. "Just shut your mouth and keep it shut!"

Kirkland looked up at the wall speakers. "What's holding things up? Listen to me," he shouted into the speakers. *"I want that ship!"*

Barry began to worry. It looked as if Kirkland stood a good chance of escaping. And if he did, Barry knew he would be in big trouble with Commander Olinda. He had not kept to a rule of the prison. He had felt sorry for Kirkland and left him alone with his brother.

Commander Olinda's voice came through the wall speakers.

"Kirkland, listen to me," she said. "I've decided not to give you the ship you want. And there's no way you can get out of the cellblock. You'll stay there until you're ready to give yourself up. I can wait."

"Maybe *you* can wait, Olinda," Kirkland said. "But what about Marks here? Can *he* wait?"

"Officer Marks is a member of the Space Police force," Commander Olinda answered. "Like the rest of us he has to take chances in his job. You do understand that, don't you, Marks?"

"Yes," Barry answered. "Don't give him the ship."

"Olinda!" Kirkland shouted. "Have you got us on your TV set?"

"Yes," said Commander Olinda. "I can see you on the set in my office."

"Good," Kirkland said. "Keep watching. This show isn't over yet."

With that, Kirkland pointed Barry's gun at Barry. Barry took a step back, his body stiff. Was Kirkland going to kill him?

As if he knew what Barry had been thinking, Kirkland said, "I'm not going to kill you, cop. I need you to help me get out of here."

Barry was glad to hear what Kirkland had said. But then, all of a sudden, Kirkland fired the gun at him.

The top of Barry's right arm was burning hot. He knew he had been hit. He also knew that Kirkland did not want to kill him. Kirkland had just wanted to hurt him. By shooting Barry, Kirkland had told Commander Olinda he meant business.

Pain ran through Barry's arm like a river of fire. He looked down. Part of his shirt was burned away. So was a small part of his arm.

"Marks!" Commander Olinda called. "I'll send the doctor in to take care of your arm."

"No, don't!" Barry said. "That will make two of us trapped in here. Kirkland would like that, you can be sure."

Barry pressed his arm with his left hand just above the place where he had been hit. This kept the blood from streaming out.

Commander Olinda spoke again through the wall speakers. "A ship is ready and waiting for you, Kirkland. Marks, take the prisoner to

Air Lock Three. He can board the ship there."

"No!" Barry shouted. "Commander, I—."

"You have your orders, Marks," Commander Olinda said. "Take the prisoner to Air Lock Three."

"You heard her," Kirkland said to Barry. "Let's go."

Barry, still holding his hurt arm, walked down the cellblock. Kirkland followed him. Barry unlocked the door at the end of the cellblock. The two men went through it. After Barry had locked the door behind him, he climbed the steps that led to the prison's docking stations.

With Kirkland right behind him, he made his way to Air Lock Three. He got there at the same time as Officer Joan Tarkoff.

"Joan!" Barry said. "Get back!"

But she didn't move. Instead she opened the air lock. To Barry she said, "I'm to fly the prisoner out of here."

"I'm sorry, Joan," Barry said. "I wish you hadn't got mixed up in this mess I've made."

Joan said, "Don't worry about me." She smiled at Barry. Then she said, "Commander Olinda told me to tell you to go to the doctor at once. She doesn't want you to waste any time."

"See you, cop," Kirkland said, and stepped into the air lock with Joan. The door closed.

Barry turned and ran for the prison's hospital. The doctor was waiting for him. He began at once to take care of Barry's arm. He didn't say anything as he worked. Barry didn't either.

When the doctor had finished, he told Barry that Commander Olinda wanted to see him. So Barry left the hospital. He made his way to Commander Olinda's office. When he got there, he waited to hear what she would say to him.

She didn't ask him to sit down as she had the first time they had met. She sat at her desk, looking at him for several seconds. Then she said, "Turn on that TV set."

Barry turned on the set.

"Get Air Lock Three. The outside dock."

Barry did as he was told. He watched the ship that was at the dock. So did Commander Olinda. Both of them saw the ship's jet fire. They watched without speaking as the ship left the dock and flew off into space.

"Turn off the set," Olinda said.

Barry did.

"That's the first time anyone has ever escaped from this prison," said Commander Olinda. "The very first time."

"What I did was wrong," Barry said. "I know I should have stayed in front of the prisoner's cell when his brother was there."

"That's right!" Commander Olinda shouted and banged her hand on the top of her desk. "You should have stayed there!"

She stood up and faced Barry. "We have rules in this prison. The rules were made for good reasons. If you had kept to the rule that says officers must watch prisoners during all visits, this would not have happened. Am I right in saying that, Marks?"

"You are."

Commander Olinda sat down again. She picked up a paper and showed it to Barry. "I don't want you working in this prison any longer," she said. "This paper is all filled in. You can see what it says, can't you?"

"Yes," Barry said. "It says that I'm to return to the planet Delta's police command."

"Today," said Commander Olinda. "There's a ship waiting to fly you out of here."

WHERE IS MORGAN?

Barry saluted Commander Olinda and left her office. In less than an hour he was ready to leave the prison. He boarded a ship at Dock Two and took off.

Barry didn't know the officer who was flying the ship. The man kept looking at him. He seemed to want to say something. But Barry hoped he wouldn't. He didn't feel at all like talking.

Finally the man at the ship's controls spoke. "I hear you're the one who let the prisoner escape."

Barry didn't answer him.

The man said, "I hear Commander Olinda fired you. Is that why you're going to Delta?"

"That's where I'm going," Barry said, without really telling the man anything.

For a few minutes the man kept his eyes on the ship's controls. Then he spoke again. "It's too bad you got on the wrong side of Olinda. She didn't get to be a commander by letting her people do things the wrong way."

Barry thought about his dream of becoming a commander in the police force. Now that dream would never come true. Too many people in the force would remember what had happened when they heard the name Officer Barry Marks.

They would say when they heard Barry's name, "Officer Marks? Isn't he the one who let a prisoner escape from the prison satellite?"

Few would remember that Barry had been a good cop for the year he had been in the force. And no matter how good he was in the years to come, people wouldn't want to take a chance on him. He might do something wrong again.

Maybe, Barry thought, I should leave the force now. Get out, find another job. But he didn't want to. He loved his job. It made him feel that he was doing something important with his life.

Through the ship's windows, Barry watched the stars fly by. The sound of the ship's radio filled his ears. Calls for help were coming in. Officers talked to one another, and ships were sent out from one part of space to another.

The radio!

Barry spoke to the man flying the ship. "Let me use the radio."

"What for? I can't let you use it for anything but police business."

"This is police business. Move over."

The man moved to one side and Barry sat down next to him. He spoke into the radio.

"This is Officer Marks. I'm calling Officer Tarkoff. Come in, please."

"Tarkoff here. What do you want, Marks?"

"Is everything OK?"

Barry heard another voice. He knew it was Kirkland's. He asked again, "Is everything OK?"

"Yes," Joan Tarkoff answered. "We're about to land on the planet Del—."

The radio went dead.

But Barry had heard enough. It was a chance. He had taken it and it had paid off. Now he knew where Kirkland was heading. To Delta.

Maybe, Barry thought, all isn't lost yet. Maybe I can do something about the mess I've made. He decided to try.

The man next to Barry asked, "What happened to your radio line?"

"The prisoner on Officer Tarkoff's ship must have cut it," Barry said.

When the ship landed on the planet Delta some time later, Barry got out. He headed for the police station where he used to work. Officer Vilma was there. "I heard what happened at the prison," Dennis Vilma said. "I'm sorry, Barry. That was bad luck for you."

Barry asked, "Can I check the computer for something?"

"It's OK with me. I mean you haven't been thrown out of the force. You're still a cop so you can use the computer."

Barry went to the computer. He asked it where Morgan Kirkland lived. The computer told him. Then Barry asked the computer to print a picture of Morgan. The computer did.

Barry took it, looked at it, and put the picture in his pocket.

"See you," Barry said to Dennis and left the station. Dennis looked after him and shook his head.

Barry had made up his mind to find Morgan. If he found Morgan he just might find Kirkland, too. So he went to Morgan's home. But when he got there, Morgan wasn't there. So Barry asked some of the neighbours about him.

"Nice young man," said the woman who lived next door.

"Clever, that one," said a man. "He knows a lot about science. He can build just about anything. In fact he mended my Air Car twice for me. Good boy, that Morgan."

Barry asked the man if he knew where Morgan was now. The man said he didn't. It was a little boy who finally told Barry what he wanted to know.

The boy said he was a friend of Morgan's. "Even little kids like me are his friends," the boy said. "Everyone is."

"I'm looking for your friend," Barry told the boy. "Do you happen to know where he is?"

The boy looked up at Barry. "Why do you want him? He didn't do anything, did he?"

"I want to talk to him about something."

"He's not here," the boy said.

"I know that. I want to know where he is. Do you know?"

"He's on holiday. He left today," the boy said.

Barry asked, "How do you know?"

"He told me he was going on holiday. I didn't believe him. So he showed me his ticket."

Barry asked the boy, "Where was he going for his holiday?"

The boy said, "To our moon."

"Thank you," Barry said.

As he started to leave, the boy called to him. "You going to the moon to see Morgan?"

"I am," Barry answered.

"When you see him, tell him I hope he comes back soon."

"I'll tell him that," Barry said. He walked off, and then started running towards the space field. There he bought a ticket for Delta's moon. During the trip to the moon, Barry did some hard thinking.

He didn't believe that Morgan had gone to the moon for a holiday. There wasn't anything to do on the moon but work. Someone had found gold on the moon a while ago. But no one had found any after that. Was Morgan going there to try to find gold?

What else did Barry know about Delta's moon? There was no Space Police station there. Many ships stopped at the moon instead of at Delta. But in the end, Barry could come up with no answer to his question. He still didn't know why Morgan had gone to Delta's moon. He thought some more.

A thought crossed his mind: What if the little boy had been wrong? What if Morgan had lied to the boy? What if he wasn't going to the moon at all? But the boy had said that Morgan had shown him his ticket.

Still, Barry thought, I might be wasting my time. But the only way to find out was to go there himself. It was a chance he had to take. It was about the only chance, he believed, to find Kirkland and bring him back to the prison.

WAITING FOR THE HOSPITAL SHIP

As soon as Barry got to Delta's moon, he began his hunt for Morgan. He showed Morgan's picture to people who worked at the space field. One woman who ran a small shop thought she had seen him but she wasn't sure.

"He would have got here today, I think," Barry told the woman.

She had another look at Morgan's picture and said she still couldn't be sure. "Maybe the kid I saw was the kid in the picture," she said. "But maybe not. Why don't you try the gold mines? If it was him I saw, he's probably out there trying to find gold."

Barry bought some miner's clothes from her. He didn't want to look like a cop. He wanted to look like just another miner. But he didn't throw away his gun.

There were no Air Cars on the moon. To get around you either had to walk or ride a zin, a strange animal found only on the moon. A zin used its two big legs to stand on. Its two tiny front legs weren't used for running or walking—just for eating. It had a long neck and eyes that burned like green fire. Barry rented a zin from the shop owner and climbed on. When he hit the zin's sides, the animal began to run.

The zin ran for a long time until Barry made it stop at a miners' camp. He got off the animal and showed the men and women in the camp Morgan's picture. None of them had seen him.

Barry was just about to leave when a woman came up out of the mine. Barry asked the woman about Morgan. The woman said that Morgan wasn't at the mine. But the woman had seen him.

Barry asked her, "Where?"

"He was at that little shop near the space field," the woman said.

"When?"

The woman said, "Today. I remember him well. He was asking a lot of questions."

"What kind of questions?"

"Oh, about what ships come to this moon. He wanted to know about the hospital ship that's going to land today. He wanted to know if it was always on time."

"Thanks," Barry said, and got back on the zin. He headed the animal back to the shop. The shop keeper was still there when Barry got back. Barry told her what the miner had said about Morgan and showed her Morgan's picture again.

"You know, you're right," said the woman. "This *is* the kid I saw. I remember now. He *was* interested in when the hospital ship was coming here."

"When *is* the hospital ship supposed to land?"

"In two hours. It stops here once a week. It takes medicine and drugs to the planets around here. It stops here to have its jets checked."

Barry thanked the woman and went back outside. Since the hospital ship was coming, he thought, Morgan should be showing up pretty soon. Barry walked over to the dock where the hospital ship would land.

Barry was right. Morgan showed up an hour before the hospital ship was supposed to land. With him were two other young men. Barry didn't like the look of them. Their eyes kept moving from one thing to another. They didn't seem to know what to do with their hands. They couldn't keep still.

Barry moved behind the building and reached down to pick up some dirt. He rubbed it on his face and hands. Now, he hoped, he looked more like a miner. He also hoped Morgan wouldn't remember him from the prison.

He walked across the road to where Morgan was standing with the two other men. "Nice day," he said. "Very nice."

He got no answer.

He asked, "Waiting for someone?"

"Just hanging about," Morgan said.

Barry asked, "Meeting the hospital ship?" He saw that Morgan almost jumped.

Barry stood to one side, looking at the three men. Then he started to walk past them. As he did he fell against one of Morgan's friends. He and the man hit the ground.

The man shouted at Barry, "What do you think you're doing?"

"Sorry," Barry said. He grabbed the man as if he wanted to help him get up. He felt the man's laser gun under his clothes.

The man said, "Get out of here, will you? Just get out."

Barry left Morgan and his friends. He went back to stand in front of the shop. From there he watched the three of them. He asked himself, what do I know now? One, those three are waiting for the hospital ship to come. Two, they're carrying guns.

Just then Barry heard the sound of a door closing behind him. He turned and saw the woman locking up her shop. The few miners who had been in it had left. Now there was no one around but Barry, Morgan, and Morgan's two friends.

Soon Morgan walked up to Barry. Morgan said, "What are you hanging around here for?"

"No special reason," Barry said. "I just kind of like it here. I hope you don't mind."

"I do mind," Morgan said. "I think it's time

for you to move on. Now get out of our way."

"OK, OK," Barry said. He held up his hands in front of him as if he were afraid of Morgan. "Don't get worked up," he said. "I was going."

"So go!"

Barry walked to the back of the shop and then began to climb the hill behind it. But he didn't climb very far. As soon as he found a place where he could hide behind some big stones, he dropped down out of sight of Morgan and his friends.

But he kept his eyes on them.

A few minutes went by. Suddenly Barry felt someone's hands around his neck. He tried to get to his feet but he couldn't. He tried to pull the hands from his neck. But they were too strong for him. Blood began to pound in his head. He couldn't see very well. Then he passed out.

When he woke up later, he was on the ground. Kirkland was standing over him.

Barry felt his side. "You took my gun," he said.

"I'm going to need it before very long," Kirkland said.

"I thought if I found Morgan I'd find you too," Barry said.

"You have a good head," said Kirkland. "But what made you think that way?"

"Everyone believes you broke out of prison to save your life," Barry said. "I'm probably the only one who doesn't think so. And I don't think so because of the way you were hitting Morgan when he came to see you."

"I told you about that," Kirkland said. "It was just a family fight."

Barry shook his head. "I think it was something more. You talked to me before Morgan visited you. You were afraid of what would happen to him when you were gone. So I asked myself why you would hit him. There had to be a good reason."

"So what's the reason, cop?"

"I don't know. Not yet. But I was right about one thing. You broke out so you could come after Morgan. The fact that you're here now tells me that."

"That's right," Kirkland said, and looked up at the sky. "Morgan told me when he visited me that he had left school. He had been studying science there. He's very good at science. That kid could be anything he wants to be. But no. He's got other ideas. He's going to be rich, Morgan is."

Barry asked, "How's he going to get rich?"

"Do you know about Flyers?"

Flyers was the name of a drug that could make you believe you were living in any world you wanted. Flyers were made by mixing two different kinds of medicine. The drug was very powerful.

"Sure. Every cop knows about Flyers," Barry said. "That drug is sold on almost all the worlds."

And then it hit Barry. Flyers were made from two different medicines. And where could you get those medicines on the moon?

"The hospital ship!" Barry said.

"That's Morgan's game, cop. He and his friends are going to steal what they need from the hospital ship. Then they're going to make and sell Flyers."

"And you're here to help them, is that it?"

Kirkland looked at him in surprise. "Help them? Far from it. I came here to stop them."

THE BROKEN RULE

Barry said, "I get it now. Morgan gave you that red machine to help you escape from prison. Then he told you what he was planning to do here on Delta's moon. That's why you hit him, isn't it? Because he was planning to steal the medicines from the hospital ship and start making and selling drugs?"

"You're right," Kirkland said. "He told me about the plan. And he wanted me to help him get the medicines. I told him no. But I knew I had to get out to stop him. I landed on Delta.

But Morgan had already come to this moon. So I followed him. I got here just before you did."

"And since then—"

"And since then," Kirkland said, "I've been watching Morgan. And waiting. I'm going to stop him when the hospital ship comes."

Barry said, "But you attacked me before. You took my gun. I thought you were trying to kill me because I was going to stop Morgan."

"I didn't want to take a chance on you shooting me," Kirkland said.

He looked up at the sky. So did Barry. A ship was there. It circled once and then landed.

"That's the hospital ship," Kirkland said. He looked down at Barry. "You'd better get up. We've got a job to do." He gave Barry's gun back to him.

Barry got up and looked down at the hospital ship. Close to it stood Morgan and his friends.

"Let's go down there," Kirkland said. "But don't start shooting, cop. Let me talk to my brother first."

Barry and Kirkland started down the hill. They had almost reached the ship when Morgan saw his brother. He let out a shout and ran up to Kirkland. "I'm so glad to see you!" he said, a happy smile on his face. "I hoped you'd change your mind."

"I'm here," Kirkland said. "But I have to talk to you."

Morgan looked at Barry. "Who's this? He was hanging around here before. I think I've seen him some place before."

Kirkland said, "Morgan, don't attack the ship."

Morgan asked, "What did you say? Not that line again."

"Don't do it," Kirkland said. "You'll end up like me. Maybe not right away. But it'll happen to you, too. Believe me. I know what I'm talking about."

Morgan turned to his friends. "Did you hear my big brother? He must think he's a cop or something." He looked back at Kirkland. "I got you out of that prison. I said we'd bring you in on this score. But you won't come in on it.

"Your brother's right," Barry said to Morgan. "You should do as he says."

"Not likely," Morgan said to Barry. "He's gone soft." Then he took a close look at Barry. "I *do* know you! And I know where I saw you! It was in the prison. You're a cop!"

At that word *cop,* Morgan's friends pulled out their guns and pointed them at Barry. Then Morgan took out his gun and looked at his brother. "*You* brought this cop here! I should fix you now! Is this the way you pay me back for what I did for you?"

"Yes," Kirkland said, "it is. I'm doing it for your own good."

One of Morgan's friends asked, "Want me to give it to the cop?"

Morgan turned round at the sound of his friend's voice. As he did, Barry grabbed him from behind and shouted, "Move, Kirkland!"

Kirkland threw himself at Morgan's friends. He grabbed them before they could move, knocking them both down. In a second he had their guns in his hands.

"It's all over," Kirkland told them.

Just then a door opened in the side of the hospital ship. A doctor came out of the ship and looked around. "What's going on here?"

"I'm a police officer," Barry said. "Everything's OK now. Can I use your radio?"

The doctor led Barry into the hospital ship. When Barry came out several minutes later, he spoke to Kirkland. "I radioed to Officer

Tarkoff. She was flying back to the prison. She's coming here now to pick us up."

Kirkland's face changed as Barry spoke. He looked down at the two guns in his hands. Then he looked at Barry. Barry knew what Kirkland was thinking. But he stood his ground. Kirkland looked at Morgan. Then he said, "I'll be ready when she gets here."

When Joan Tarkoff landed her ship on the moon some time later, Kirkland forced Morgan and his friends to get on it. Then he and Barry boarded the ship. A few minutes later, when she had a chance, Joan whispered to Barry, "What happened? How did Kirkland get those guns? Why don't you take them away from him?"

As Joan flew the ship into space, Barry answered all her questions. He told her what had happened. When they got back to the prison, Kirkland handed over his guns. Then Barry and Joan put him in a cell. Next they locked up Morgan and his friends.

As Joan and Barry were about to leave the cellblock, Kirkland called Barry's name. Barry went over to him. Kirkland asked him to do something for him.

"I don't know if I can," Barry said. "It's against prison rules." His face had a questioning look on it. Then he left the cellblock and went to Commander Olinda's office. Before he could knock, she opened the door.

The two of them looked at one another for a minute without speaking. Then Commander Olinda smiled.

"Come in," she said. "I know a little bit about what happened. When Officer Tarkoff got your call, she radioed me. She told me she was going to pick up you and your prisoners on Delta's moon. I saw you on the TV set as you put the men in their cells. Tell me the rest of the story."

Barry told her everything that had happened since he left the prison. When he finished Commander Olinda shook her head. Then she said, "I seem to have lost that paper that said you were to go back to work on Delta. I don't plan to look for it now."

Barry asked, "Then I'm to work here in the prison?"

"You are, Captain Marks," Commander Olinda said.

"Captain Marks? Did you say *Captain* Marks?"

"I did."

Barry thought of his dream of becoming a commander in the Space Police. That dream was now one big step nearer to coming true thanks to Commander Olinda.

"There's one thing I wanted to ask you," Barry said. "Kirkland asked me to do something for him. But it's against the rules."

"Oh, no, Marks!" Commander Olinda said. "Not again. You're still breaking rules?"

"No," Barry said. "Not if you think I shouldn't." He told her what Kirkland wanted.

The next morning, Morgan stood before the TV set in Commander Olinda's office. Barry stood next to him. Commander Olinda sat behind her desk. She spoke to Morgan. "Only police officers can watch an execution. But your brother Kirkland wanted you to see his execution. So I broke my own rule and had Captain Marks bring you here."

"It's time now," Barry said. He looked at Morgan. "Your brother wanted it this way, just as Commander Olinda said. Morgan, he wants only the best for you. He wants you to know— to see what happens to people who murder other people."

"He didn't mean to kill that woman," Morgan said in a soft voice.

"I know he didn't," Barry said. "But the fact is he did kill her. And he wants to be sure you don't end up doing the same thing."

Barry saluted Commander Olinda and left her office. He went to the cellblock. At Kirkland's cell, he stopped. "It's time, Kirkland."

"What about Morgan?"

"He's in the commander's office. The TV set is on."

"Thanks, cop," Kirkland said. "And so long."

Barry pressed the first of the two buttons outside Kirkland's cell. A wall came down in front of it. Then Barry pressed the second button.

He left the cellblock and returned to Commander Olinda's office. He stood next to Morgan and watched the television set. On it he could see Kirkland floating far into space. He looked away from the set and saw that Morgan was trying very hard not to cry.

Commander Olinda got up and turned off the set. "Return this prisoner to the cellblock, Marks," she said. Barry led Morgan from her office.

On the way back to his cell, Morgan looked at Barry. "He wanted me to see him die so that I'd—know."

"He loved you very much," Barry said. "My guess is that the computer won't give you more than a year here for helping your brother escape. After that it's all up to you. You could go back to school and study science again. Make something of yourself. I hope you will. I hope you'll remember what your brother wanted for you."

"I will," Morgan said. "I promise you I will." He went into his cell. Barry locked the door.